Rosie,
Who Thought She Was a
BIG DOG

Archway Publishing books may be ordered through booksellers or by contacting:

Archway Publishing
1663 Liberty Drive
Bloomington, IN 47403
www.archwaypublishing.com
844.669.3957

Illustrated by Paula Velazquez Limbaugh
and Brynn E. Limbaugh

ISBN: 978-1-4808-9672-7 (sc)
ISBN: 978-1-4808-9671-0 (e)

Print information available on the last page.

Archway Publishing rev. date: 10/05/2020

Rosie,
Who Thought She Was a
BIG DOG

Hey Milo.
Hope you enjoy the story
about Rosie who lived across
the street from Grannes +
Grandpa. Enjoy!
Ramona A. Velazquez

Ramona A. Velazquez

Dogs come in all sizes. Some are big. Some are medium. Some are small. This story is about a small dog who thought she was a big dog.

Rosie was born the runt of the litter. Her mother was a medium-sized dog. Her sisters were medium-sized dogs. But Rosie was very small.

The dogs all lived happily with the Mckray family in Mexico, where Mr. and Mrs. Mckray chose to retire.

Their small house had a big porch and lots of land. There was an old shed located next to the fence in their front yard. A few feet from the shed, there was a gate that was shaped to look like a sea turtle. The gate opened to a very long driveway, which led to the house. In their yard were giant cactuses and large palm trees. There was no grass, just lots of raked sand. The sand helped them spot snakes that might be passing through their yard. It was the perfect house for dogs to live in. It was the perfect house for the Mckrays to retire in.

BELimbaug

Rosie's sisters and mother looked very much alike. They all had curly white fur and pointed noses. When they barked, it could be described as yapping. They were fast runners, but Rosie was the fastest.

When Mrs. Mckray called the dogs to dinner, she could count on Rosie being the first one to the food. When her sisters tried to push her out of the way, they found it impossible. She stood her ground. They had to move to other spots around the giant bowl.

When Mr. Mckray yelled for the dogs to chase the donkeys out of his yard, Rosie got there first, barking at the donkeys and nipping at their hooves. She never ran away when a donkey charged her. She charged the donkey right back until that donkey left. Rosie may have been a small dog, but she thought she was a big dog.

When it was bedtime for the Mckrays, all the dogs, except for their mother, curled up on the sofa on the front porch. Their mother slept inside with the Mckrays, as she had always done. They did this every night, even on rainy nights.

But one night was different. Rosie and her sisters, as usual, were huddled together on their sofa outside while the Mckrays and their mother slept inside. They were all dozing off when out of nowhere a large coyote, followed by two smaller coyotes, leaped over the fence and quietly stood by the porch, staring.

When the dogs looked up, they were so scared that they jumped off the sofa and began to scatter in all directions—all of them, that is, except Rosie. She stood her ground on the porch, staring back at the coyotes.

Rosie's frightened sister Pearl caught the eye of the biggest coyote when she ran to the small tool shed by the gate.

The large coyote wasted no time running after her. In an instant, the other two smaller coyotes joined him. Now the three coyotes surrounded Pearl as she leaned up against the shed, trapped. Pearl began to shake with fear.

In a flash, Rosie ran to the shed and placed herself between the coyotes and her sister. The coyotes were surprised by the move but began to lick their lips.

"Two is better than one," growled the leader as he smiled at Rosie. The coyotes cautiously moved in on their prey. What they didn't know and weren't prepared for was Rosie, a small dog who thought she was a big dog.

Rosie began with a deep growl. The coyotes stopped and stared. That big growl surprised them. Then Rosie began to bark loudly and frantically. Her other two sisters, who were hiding behind the house, heard her and joined in barking. Mother Dog could hear her pups and began barking next to Mr. Mckray's head. There was barking in the house and around the yard, waking Mr. and Mrs. Mckray.

Meanwhile, back at the shed, Rosie lunged quickly at the leader of the pack and nipped his paw, just as she had done with the donkeys. The leader was so surprised that he stopped in his tracks. Then Rosie charged her head into the chest of the leader, throwing him backwards. The coyote was hurt. The other two coyotes just watched, frozen and not sure what to do next.

Ping! Ping! Something hit the shed. The coyotes turned and looked toward the porch at Mr. Mckray. He was firing steel balls from a slingshot at the coyotes.

Ping! Ping! Ping! A steel ball hit one of the coyotes and sent him running.

Ping! The next coyote watched the steel ball just miss his face. He didn't wait around. He took off for the gate next to the shed, with the leader of the pack close behind. Leaping the gate put all three coyotes back on the road, and they ran until they disappeared into the darkness.

"Here, girls! On the porch now!" Mr. Mckray waved his slingshot while calling for the dogs. The dogs heard him call and ran from their hiding places in back to where he was standing on the porch. Rosie, caring for her frightened sister, pushed Pearl toward Mr. Mckray, who was now sitting on the porch sofa covered in dogs.

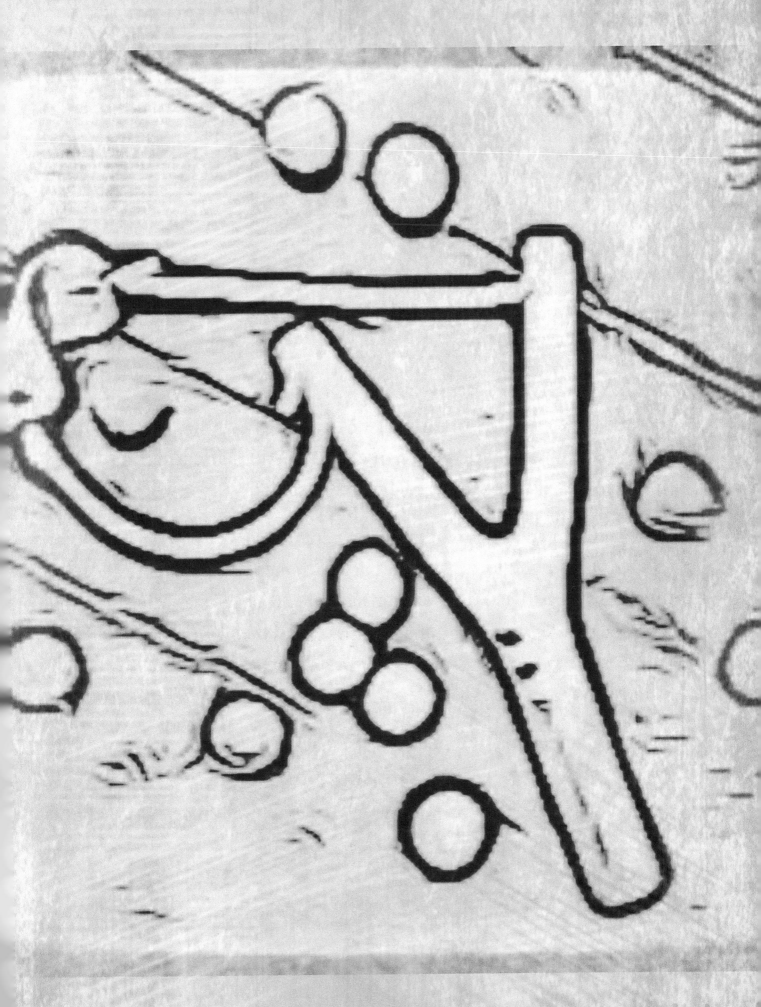

While all the dogs were gathered around Mr. Mckray, the screen door opened, and out came Mrs. Mckray, followed by the dogs' mother. Mrs. Mckray pulled the belt on her robe tightly around her as she stepped onto the porch.

"Are those coyotes gone? Oh my gosh! I can't believe that hungry pack didn't leave with one of our pups. We're so lucky." Mrs. Mckray's voice was cracking; she was holding back tears as she said those words.

Mr. Mckray smiled at her while he was petting Rosie. "It wasn't luck. It was Rosie. She is the leader of *this* pack. She kept those coyotes at bay until help could arrive. She saved her sister Pearl. Thank goodness Rosie doesn't let her size stop her. She may be a small dog, but she thinks she is a big dog."

All the dogs seemed to know what Mr. Mckray was saying. They wagged their tails in agreement and bent down to lick Rosie's face.

And so Rosie, the smallest dog in the group, was a hero to her family and to the Mckrays. Mrs. Mckray rewarded Rosie with her favorite thing in the whole world, a squirt of whipped cream in a bowl. After licking the bowl and her lips, Rosie walked to a spot on the porch in front of her sisters. Her sisters wagged their tails in unison. They felt protected with Rosie there. After all, Rosie may have been the smallest dog, but she thought she was the biggest dog.

It's not how others see you that's important. It's how you see yourself!